MISCHIEVOUS MIMI

The Cats of Dragon Hill

3

MISCHIEVOUS MIMI

Sue Holland

For Meg

CHAPTER 1

Gunner raced through the allotments at high speed, he pretended he was being chased by a ferocious dog; it was good practice for when he was. Gunner still held the title for the fastest cat on Dragon Hill, a title that he wanted to hold onto for as long as he could. He slowed down so he could clamber over the fence. As he landed, he felt a sharp stabbing pain. Ouch, he thought as he stopped to look down at his leg. That hurt. He looked back and saw the broken and jagged fence which had caused the trouble. Gunner gave the wound a quick lick then bounded on towards Dragon Hill.

But what was going on? What was that noise? Gunner paused. His curious ears pricked up. He could hear humans shouting

– in fact, not just shouting, shrieking! Dragon Hill was usually a peaceful place but not today. His lean ginger-striped body sprinted up the road towards the cherry tree, his sore leg now forgotten. He came to a halt outside Mimi's house.

'You naughty, naughty cat,' heard Gunner. 'We're so disappointed in your behaviour, Mimi. Go away and think about what you've done. Shoo!'

Gunner watched as Mimi was chased out of the house by her owners. He could see a flash of white running towards him. What did she have all over her face?

'Is that cream, Mimi?' asked Gunner. 'You've done it again, haven't you?' he scolded.

'I'm afraid I've been an incy, wincy bit naughty,' she said, trying to blink through the cream.

'C'mon Mimi, let's go down to the skate park and you can sort your face out.'

'Let's sit here Mims,' Gunner continued. 'We can watch the children do their tricks and stunts. Cor, look at that one!'

Mimi started to lick the cream from her face.

'So, what did you do this time? As if I needed to ask…'

'Well, the thing is Gunner,' she said, in between licks. 'It's not as awful as last week when I leapt up at the delivery driver and made him shriek. You see, my owners, Simon and Louise, are throwing a small party this afternoon and Louise, she gets called Lou for short—'

'Yes, yes, get on with it Mimi,' said Gunner, wagging his tail impatiently.

'Okay, sorry. Anyway, where was I? Ah yes, the party. I don't like it when they have these parties. Humans come into my home and start stroking me and one annoying little human, he's called Claude, always turns up, come rain or shine, and he just loves to tug on my tail, then dribbles all over me. And do you know what? Today he even tried to sit on me! He said, Come on horsey, faster! Then he mopped his nose with the back of his hand and wiped all this green slimy stuff all over my fur! Look Gunner, can you see it?'

Gunner looked down at Mimi's fur. The slimy trail glistening in the sunshine.

Gunner nodded sympathetically. 'Then what?'

'So, there it was Gunner – an irresistible, freshly-made trifle with ever-so-slightly-warm custard and a luscious topping of fresh cream beautifully piped in a mesmerizing swirl. I wish you could have seen it. Lou had just put it in the fridge for this afternoon. And by the way, this cream is delicious, do you want to try some?'

'Well, what happened next?' asked Gunner.

'The thing is, a few months ago, I found out I could do this amazing trick. I can slide my paw under the fridge door and PING – I can pull it open! Just like that. Oh, you should have seen the delights on offer, Gunner! But I had my sights set firmly on that trifle.'

'Mimi! How could you?'

'Well, you see, it isn't entirely my fault. I've been feeling upset lately, almost angry in fact. Simon and Lou have taken my favourite Tricky Treats away and they've replaced them with these new snacks which are, to be honest, quite horrid.'

'Your owners must have been very annoyed. In fact, I know they were, I heard them shouting from the bottom of Dragon Hill!'

'You've got to help me Gunner. I need to stop being so naughty. I never used to be like this. That's why we had to move house you see – I upset the neighbours.'

'I'm glad you came to Dragon Hill Mimi. But what sort of things did you do?'

'Oh, nothing that awful. Just the usual. Opening the wheelie bins when the neighbours were asleep at night and dragging out the leftovers. It's great fun, Gunner, throwing bits of food in the air, then whacking them hard with your paw. The sprouts fly the furthest! One landed on a neighbour's conservatory roof, three doors away. Tea bags are my favourite though. Especially when they burst open and all the tea leaves sprinkle out and flutter down like snow. But I do understand why they were so cross about the 'Raised Bed Incident'.'

'The Raised Bed Incident?!' shouted Gunner.

'The neighbours had new raised vegetable beds in their garden. They filled them with wonderfully soft compost; it felt so good under my paws and really easy to dig. They spent ages planting the seedlings – broccoli, spring onions, lettuce and carrots. The soil was just perfect for a toilet, I couldn't have wished for better.'

'MIMI! I'm not surprised they were angry with you. You can't go round weeing wherever you fancy. You really do need my help, don't you?'

'Yes, Gunner, I really do.'

CHAPTER 2

On Monday evening, Gunner met Mimi at the allotments. They were off to the clubhouse for a meeting.

'I'm looking forward to tonight, Mimi. It's been a while.'

'It will feel strange without the others.'

'Well, we have a new cat joining us tonight,' said Gunner.

'Oh yes, who's that?'

'An old friend of mine – Agatha. She's a wise and clever cat you know, but I had better warn you, she does have this one strange habit.'

'What's that then?'

'She loves Shakespeare,' said Gunner.

'What's Shakespeare? Some kind of kitty treat?'

13

'Shakespeare was a famous human, Mimi. Famous for writing plays and also for his quotes. Agatha loves nothing more than to recite them.'

'I know a Shakespeare quote!'

'I don't think you do.'

'I do! If it ain't broke, don't fix it.'

Gunner chuckled. 'Well, almost. Come on, I'll race you,' he called out, already half way across the allotments.

Gunner was first to enter the clubhouse. He went in through the back window and into the kitchen. He breathed in the familiar musty smell. It seemed stronger than before, probably because it had been empty for a while. As he entered the next room, he glanced over at the gold chair, Sheba's favourite, where she spent many an hour grooming her white fur until it was pristine.

It was very quiet without her and Felix. He never thought he would miss their bickering.

Sheba had moved with her owners to France for the warmer weather. She had told Gunner that she would be coming back later in the year but Gunner wasn't so sure. What if her owners liked it so much in France that they decided to stay? And Felix had moved to the coast. His owners had always wanted to live by the sea. He was probably tucking into a bowl of tasty fresh fish at this very moment.

There was a gentle tap on the front window of the clubhouse.

'Come on in Agatha,' welcomed Gunner, opening the door. 'This is Mimi.'

Agatha walked over to the gold chair. 'May I?'

'Oh, please do, we saved that seat especially for you,' said Gunner.With her soft grey fur and olive-green eyes, Agatha jumped onto the chair.

'But tell me Gunner,' said Agatha, 'I'd heard that Felix moved away, but where is Sheba? I haven't seen her in a while.'

'Sheba is in France for the summer. Her owners have bought a chateau there. She seemed very happy about it and couldn't wait to leave,' sighed Gunner, recalling that she had been wearing her most elegant outfit with matching pink beret as they said farewell.

'Remember this Gunner, All that glitters is not gold,' said Agatha.

'She's probably sitting on the top step of the grand chateau entrance, grooming herself in the sunshine, then bossing the gardener around.'

'I expect you're right,' said Agatha. 'So, what's on the agenda for tonight?'

'First things first. As I came into the clubhouse tonight, I couldn't help but notice the smell,' said Gunner, sniffing the air.

'Me too,' chipped in Mimi.

'I think we should give the clubhouse a jolly good clean, get rid of the smelly sacking and find new seating. Just think how happy Sheba will be when she returns.'

'Yes, a good old tidy is exactly what the clubhouse needs,' agreed Agatha. 'I'll start in the kitchen.'

'Shall we put on some music?' asked Gunner.

'If music be the food of love, play on,' replied Agatha.

CHAPTER 3

The next day Gunner was at the allotments. He spotted Mimi walking down the road towards him.

That's odd, he thought. She's leaving black paw prints behind.

'Hi Gunner.' Mimi's whiskers twitched and then she let out an enormous sneeze.

'Your face looks strange. It looks even blacker than normal today. What's happened?'

Mimi looked guilty.

'And why is there black dust falling off you? You're going to have to tell me.'

'Well, you see, the chimney sweep came and he was emptying all the soot and... something happened. My tail started to twitch and that's when I do naughty things.

I really can't help it Gunner. But this time I may have blown it. As I came back down from the chimney, Lou shouted at me.'

'What did she say?'

'She said I had ruined the new cream carpet and if I carry on like this, I'm going to have to be re-homed!'

Gunner gulped. 'Oh dear. Does your tail twitch every time?'

'Yes,' said Mimi, 'and I have this restless feeling that won't go away.'

'Right, let's try this. When that feeling comes on and your tail starts to twitch, count to ten slowly. By the time you get to ten, the feeling should have disappeared.'

'Okay Gunner, I'll try that.'

'Actually Mimi, better make it twenty.'

That evening Gunner went up to the clubhouse with some new sacking from the allotments. He started moving things around and after a while he began to talk to himself. He pretended that Sheba was there. She was a good listener. 'So, the thing is Sheba, I want to help Mimi, but she has to help herself too. Do you think that there is something wrong or does she just love being naughty?' Gunner started sweeping. 'And to tell you the truth, I'm feeling miserable without you and Felix.'

Gunner imagined what Felix would say, 'You shouldn't keep talking to yourself Gunner, but then again, if you need expert advice…'

And what about Sheba, what would she say? 'The thing is Gunner, feelings are just visitors, let them come, then let them go.'

'Oh, yes, just visitors. Thank you for that Sheba, I rather like that.' Gunner hastily put away the broom. He'd probably done enough tidying for one evening.

Gunner sat at the skatepark. He watched the children perform tricks on their bikes and scooters, climbed a few trees and raced around the track, showing off his speed and agility. But now he was bored. He gave himself a long groom. As he washed the top of his leg, he noticed a soft lump.

Oh dear, he thought, not another cyst. It must have been when I caught my leg on the broken fence at the allotments.He hoped his owners wouldn't spot it, if they did, he would be whisked off to the vet for one of those painful and annoying jabs.

It was a long time until supper, Gunner had only just had his breakfast. He decided to walk up Dragon Hill to the cherry tree.

As he neared Mimi's house, he heard

shouting. The front door suddenly opened. Mimi was placed firmly on the step by Lou and Simon, her owners. Gunner felt the breeze on his face from the front door as it was forcefully slammed shut behind her.

'Oh dear,' said Gunner. 'The plan didn't work, did it?'

Mimi shook her head.

'Let's go for a walk, Mims.'

'Oh Gunner! The plumber came, you see, and all the floorboards were up while he fitted the new heating. I tried to ignore him and carry on eating my new snacks, which I found rather difficult as they taste quite odd. Anyway, I got distracted – I was just so curious to see what was underneath the house. But then my tail started to twitch! I counted to twenty like you said, and I thought it was working but the naughtiness seemed to take over, like a curse. I shot under the floorboards and had a good look about, but then I got stuck! Lou had to come and rescue me. She lost her torch and was covered from head to toe in cobwebs and dirt.'

'Oh Mimi, haven't you heard of that saying, Curiosity killed the cat?'

'Is that Shakespeare too?'

'Erm…'

'She also shouted something odd at me,' added Mimi.

'What was that?'

'She said I had to put it back right away. But put what back? What did she mean, Gunner?'

'Right, a Plan B is needed. Follow me!' Gunner marched towards the allotments while Mimi tried to keep up.

'Not so fast, my legs are shorter than yours,' she called out.

'Now Mimi,' said Gunner, coming to a halt. 'Find a big space around you.'

'Well, that's easy. There's only us here.'

'Now, stretch both paws over your head and lower your body down to the ground. Exhale at the same time.'

Mimi did as she was told. After a minute she twisted her head towards Gunner. 'Why are we doing these weird stretches?'

'They are not weird stretches Mimi. This is yoga and deep breathing. It is going to stop you from being naughty. My owner does this all the time when she's wound up.'

'And does it work?' Mimi asked. 'Oh, by the way Gunner, did you know you have a cyst on your leg?'

'Stop talking. Breathe in slowly… fill your

lungs… hold up your head… now breath out again. How does that feel?'

'I definitely feel more relaxed, Gunner. Thank you. That was a good plan. After all, Nothing ventured, nothing gained.'

'That's not Shakespeare by the way.'

'Are you sure?'

'Now don't forget, when you get that feeling, or your tail starts to twitch, start the yoga and deep breathing immediately.'

'Okay Gunner, will do.'

CHAPTER 4

That evening, Gunner decided to pay Agatha a visit. It had been a while since he had ventured past the allotments and the skatepark. As he approached the cottage where she lived, he spotted her sitting in the lavender, catching the last of the sun's rays.

'Gunner, how nice! Did you come all this way just to see me? Come and sit down.'

Gunner settled down next to the soft grey tabby.

'I always feel relaxed whilst sitting here; it's my favourite spot in the whole of the garden,' she said, almost closing her olive-green eyes.

Gunner took a sniff of the lavender. It made his nose twitch. He then started to fidget – he didn't find relaxing very easy.

'I was wondering Agatha, why have you decided to return to the clubhouse? Are you lonely?'

'No, not at all, my dear Gunner, for I have my Shakespeare for company.I just thought it would be nice to see everyone again, and perhaps Sheba will return one day.'

'Yes, I do hope so. Goodnight, Agatha.'

'Good night, good night! Parting is such sweet sorrow, that I shall say good night till it be morrow.'

Gunner trotted down to the end of the garden before galloping off in the direction of the clubhouse. He didn't usually go there at night but he was bored and not yet tired enough for sleep. As he approached, his eyes grew wider. He could see a shadow of a cat inside the clubhouse! Could it be Sheba? Perhaps she was back. On the other hand, it could be Rosco, the mean cat! He had to go and see. He had to know who was walking around in his clubhouse at this time of night.

Gunner trod silently, avoiding the crunchy twigs which lay under the oak tree and around to the back of the clubhouse. He jumped in through the kitchen window. Gunner gulped, perhaps this wasn't such a good idea after all. He already had one injury, he didn't want to risk getting another.

But hang on though, he thought. 'I didn't come this far to only come this far.'

Crikey, I sounded just like Agatha then, thought Gunner to himself.

The moving around had stopped. The other cat had clearly heard him. Gunner leapt into the other room. 'Who's there?' he called out.

'Cor, it's only you Gunner, you really spooked me.'

'Darth! What are you doing here? I haven't seen you around for ages.' Darth was a large and friendly, long-haired black-and-white cat, who lived around the corner on Church Street. Gunner looked at his emerald-green eyes and sighed when he saw Darth's fur. It was matted in quite a few places; he looked a sorry sight.

'Do you still live round the corner with your owners?'

'Well, here's the thing Gunner, you didn't see anyone else out there, did you?'

'Like who?'

'They're after me!'

'Who's after you, Darth?'

'The little humans who I live with of course. Gracie pushes me around in her doll's pram all day and Ethan wants to get rid of my matted fur. He's been following me around with that prickly hairbrush, it's like a hedgehog on a stick, but worse, much worse!'

'Ah, I see. Is Ethan the little human who loves Star Wars?'

'That's the one alright. Can I hang out here for a while?'

'Course you can Darth, no problem, but won't they be worried about you? And it's not a bad idea to let Ethan brush your coat. They are very fond of you Darth, much better than your previous owners. They didn't care for you at all! They just went off and left you for days.'

'Mm, you do have a point there. Cor Gunner, did you know you've got a big old cyst on your leg? Look at that, it's all squishy,' said Darth, moving over for a better look. 'Do you want me to burst it for you?'

'NO, I certainly do not!'

'But it's so big! I could use it as a trampoline!'

'Goodnight, Darth, I'll be seeing you tomorrow.'

CHAPTER 5

The next morning Gunner took a shortcut through the park on his way to meet Mimi. There was a mini human in the swing going very high – much too high! There was a gasp from the owner as she slowed the swing.

'Weee, wanna go high!' squealed the mini human with excitement.

'I think that's high enough,' replied the owner frowning. She looked around to see if anyone else was there. She hadn't pushed the swing that high.

But who had been pushing the swing? Gunner spotted the nearby shrub moving. Something was in there, what was it? Oh no! He could see a black tail twitching.

He marched straight to the allotments and waited impatiently for Mimi. His tail thumped angrily on the ground.

A few minutes later, Mimi came running over.

'Hey Gunner, it's a no brainer! ' she called out.

'What is a no brainer?' he replied sharply.

'It's a Shakespeare quote.'

'No, Mimi, it's not, it's definitely not.' Gunner sighed. 'I know what you've been up to, I saw your tail under the shrub.'

'But the human was having fun, Gunner, he liked being pushed high. Didn't you hear him laughing?'

Gunner shook his head. 'The yoga didn't work, did it?'

'No,' said Mimi, looking down at the ground. Gunner turned around and saw Darth sitting just behind them. His long black-and-white fur blowing gently in the breeze.

'You need to change the plan Gunner but not the goal. It's obvious that this plan isn't working,' said Darth.

'Hmm, I think you're right,' said Gunner. 'C'mon, let me show you round the neighbourhood while you're here, it's a bit different these days. And ah! You haven't met Mimi, have you?'

'Ah, Mimi! At last, I get to finally meet you.'

'Hi Darth, Gunner's told me all about–you–'

'Sorry to interrupt but let's get going. I'm getting bored with just hanging about,' said Gunner, jumping up.

'Are you coming Mims?'

'Yes please, I don't fancy going back home yet, that annoying little human is there with his owner.'

'I know exactly how annoying little humans can be, but he can't be that bad can he?' asked Darth.

'He's bad alright, but Lou thinks he's so wonderful. Claude this and Claude that, and why can't you behave like Claude, Mimi?'

Mimi followed on behind the other two cats.

'Well Darth, this is the allotments, I'm sure you'll remember these, they are pretty much the same. Nice bit of human-watching if the mood takes your fancy. Keep up Mimi. And here we are at the skatepark.'

The cats watched the children whizzing past on their bikes and enjoyed watching a girl launch off from the hill and do tricks in the air on her scooter. 'And that's one of my favourite spots there, that hill. You get a lovely view of the sun rising first thing in the morning.'

Two smaller humans came over and started to stroke Darth.

'He's very beautiful, isn't he Charlie? His eyes are so green.'

My eyes are green too, thought Gunner. Maybe not such a pretty green.

'Right, next stop, the bungalow,' said Gunner. 'It's empty at the mo, awaiting new humans. We've had some right characters live there, I can tell you. There was this mean cat called Rosco. See my tail?' Gunner held up his shortened tail and swung it from side to side. 'He did that. Then there was this Russian princess who, it turned out, wasn't from Russia at all! And believe me, she was no princess. But I'll tell you about them some other time.'

CHAPTER 6

'I like the new seating Gunner. You've done a proper job here. Just going to test it out,' said Mimi, prodding at the new sacking with her paw in the clubhouse.

Gunner held the door open for Agatha, with Darth trotting in close behind.

'Mmm, smells a lot better in here, well done everyone. That was a good plan to spring clean,' said Agatha as she made herself comfortable against one of the new cushions.

'I think Sheba will be most impressed when she returns from France,' said Gunner.

'So, what's on the agenda for tonight?' asked Agatha. 'Repairing the broken fence piece at the allotments maybe? That seems most important after what happened to your leg, Gunner.'

'Good thought Agatha, but there's something more pressing. It's Mimi, I feel we can't move on until we've helped her.'

Agatha listened intently, blinking her deep olive-green eyes frequently, as Gunner told her everything they had tried so far.

'And I've been thinking about what Darth said,' said Gunner. 'Change the plan, not the goal. The goal is definitely to help Mimi conquer her problem before it's too late.'

'Hmm, change the plan, I see,' said Agatha, tapping her paw on the arm of the chair whilst thinking. 'There is one thing we could try, but I don't know how you would feel about it, Mimi?'

'I'm desperate, Agatha. Lou and Simon are so fed up with me, I'll try anything.'

'Okay then, how do you feel about hypnotism?'

'Hypno-what?' blurted out Gunner, looking most alarmed. 'Don't know if I like the sound of that.'

'Me neither,' said Darth.

All three cats now stared at Mimi.

Mimi gulped. 'I'm not sure I want to go through with this.'

'But you have to give it a try Mimi. You don't really have any choice, do you?' said Gunner.

'To be, or not to be is the question,' said Agatha. 'Do you want to be hypnotised or not?'

Mimi nodded reluctantly.

'Right then, let's get on with it before you change your mind.' Agatha made a comfortable bed for Mimi to lie on. 'Just breathe in and out, slowly.'

'Oh, this is okay. It's just like yoga!'

'Be quiet and concentrate,' insisted Agatha. 'In and out, just relax. Are you feeling sleepy?'

Mimi didn't answer; she was already fast asleep.

'And wake up Mimi!' said Agatha.

'Huh! What happened, where am I?'

'It's alright Mims, you're fine.'

'Shall we get going now, Gunner? I think it's time we headed off home.'

'So, what happened to me?' asked Mimi as the two cats made their way back to Dragon Hill.

'Not much at all. Bit of a let-down really. Agatha took you back to when you were a kitten and said if your tail starts to twitch, you will just walk away and stay calm. And then she woke you up.'

'Oh, is that all?'

'Yep, bit boring really. I was expecting bigger and better.'

'Like what Gunner? What were you expecting?'

'That we'd find out you once lived with a magician and that you could turn cats and humans into warty toads.'

'Oh, if only that had been true. Then I could turn Claude into a toad. Just imagine!'

'Let's just keep our paws crossed and hope that Agatha's hypnotism worked.'

'Tell you something though, Gunner, I feel wonderfully relaxed and refreshed after the hypnotism. In fact, I feel like a new cat!'

'You do seem to have a spring in your step, Mims.'

'But we might have to wait a while to see if it has worked.'

'Why's that?'

'I'm off to Linda's Luxury Cat Hotel tomorrow, Gunner.'

'Again? Are Simon and Lou off on holiday?'

'I'm not sure. It's all a bit strange.'

'What makes you say that?'

'Well, they normally take me to Linda's when they go away but they haven't taken the bags out of the wardrobe and they haven't even packed anything!'

'Nothing at all? Not even a toothbrush?'

'I think they're fed up with me being naughty all the time. And Lou keeps saying that I have to bring them back but I don't know what she means. I heard her talking on the phone to another human, she said she had turned the house upside down looking for them, and that I must have hidden them. They want me gone, Gunner! What if they leave me at Linda's and don't bring me home?!'

Gunner felt lost without Mimi and wished that he could have gone to the cat hotel too. He was missing Felix and Sheba. He was never bored when they were around. He went down to the allotments and watched the humans. They were digging, weeding and chatting to each other. He didn't have anyone to chat to today. He went over to the skatepark. Children were having fun on their scooters and skateboards, but it just wasn't the same on his own without his friends.

Gunner made his way over to the clubhouse. He jumped in through the window and found Darth on the gold chair, tugging at his matted fur, trying for the umpteenth time to untangle it.

'Hey, Darth, didn't expect to find you here, thought you'd be at home. Fancy some company?'

'Sure, why not, I'm fighting a losing battle here. Shall we have a game of hide-and-seek? In fact, I'm the king of hide-and-seek – I always win.'

'Mmm, maybe later, how about exploring instead? There's plenty I haven't shown you yet.'

'You're bored, aren't you Gunner? Goodness, your cyst is looking pretty big, I think it's time that you went to the vet.'

'Nah, it'll be fine, you'll see. Come on,

let's go.' Gunner led the way as the two friends went for a stroll around the town.

'…this is the butchers, and this is the hairdressers where Vinnie used to live,' said Gunner, pointing at the window as they went past.

Gunner stopped.

'What's up Gunner? You're staring at me.'

'I just wanted to say that it's nice to have a new friend.'

Darth looked behind him. 'You mean me?'

'Of course, I mean you. I like having you around.'

'Me too. Come on, I'll race you back to the clubhouse. Last one back is a big softie.'

CHAPTER 7

Two days later, Gunner excitedly ran round and round his garden then up and down Dragon Hill as fast as he could, then bounded across the road and down Sheba's path, stopping only for a moment to sharpen his claws on the gate post in frenzied excitement.

'Hey Sheebs! I missed you,' he called out. Sheba was sitting serenely on her veranda.

'Bonjour, darling! Comment ça va?'

Gunner stood back and looked at Sheba. 'Comma what?' he replied. She looked different.

'I know what you're thinking, Gunner, that I look different. More sophisticated. That's what living in France does for you. You may as well make yourself comfortable, I'm going to tell you all about Paris – the humans, the weather, the fashion, but I think I'll start with the glorious chateau. You just wouldn't believe what fun it was!'

On Monday evening, Gunner and Sheba made their way to the clubhouse. As soon as it came into view, Sheba stopped.

'Darling, I don't remember the clubhouse being that small. I suppose it just looks tiny after living in le chateau for six months.'

Gunner growled and wagged his tail. 'I don't mind you being snobby, Sheba, but there is something I do mind.'

'And what's that, darling?'

'DON'T CALL ME DARLING. It's not good for my street cred,' he snapped, glancing around to make sure nobody had heard.

'Gunner wait! What on earth is that on your leg? Is that a cyst?'

Gunner looked at his leg. 'This is Jimmy.'

'You've given your cyst a name?'

'Well, he's been with me for quite a while now, kinda getting used to the old boy.'

Sheba peered hard at Gunner's leg. 'But it's so big. Look it's all squishy. Do you want me to burst it for you?'

'No, of course I don't, and you're the second cat who's asked me that. It's getting rather annoying. Anyone would think they'd never seen a cyst before. Now let's get going, we're late!'

The two cats rushed on to the clubhouse.

'Oh, hello Agatha, and Darth! I haven't seen you for a while,' said Sheba. She stared at Darth's face, then let her eyes cast down to his matted fur. 'Hmm,' she said. 'Unfortunate fur, darling.'

Darth narrowed his eyes and glared at

her. 'Sheba, it's so nice to see you again, I think!'

'Hello, Sheba. Did you enjoy your stay in France?' asked Agatha.

'Oh yes, I did indeed. It was amazing. The chateau was simply divine and it had a huge swimming pool.'

'You said it was a disappointing plunge pool,' interrupted Gunner.

'Well, I didn't really notice. I don't like the water anyway.'

Sheba looked around at the clubhouse. 'I think we need to rename the clubhouse, something more sophisticated, French even. How about Club Le Chat? And the room looks different... it smells different too. Not sure if I like the changes. And it's just so... you know... tiny, after the chateau.'

Agatha glared across the room at Sheba.

'How sharper than a serpent's tooth it is to have a thankless child!'

Meanwhile, over at Linda's Luxury Cat Hotel, Mimi had settled in and found a new favourite wee spot in the garden, just behind the log store. She wanted to go over and play with the young cats on the lawn but they looked quite mischievous and she couldn't risk getting into further trouble. She went over and sat under the office window which was slightly open. She could hear Simon and Lou still talking to Linda.

'We have a special occasion at our house this weekend and couldn't risk another incident. We've brought in Mimi's basket and her bowl and here are her food and snacks. We'll contact you about her collection, only… we're not sure exactly when that will be.'

That night Mimi couldn't sleep. Her supper earlier had given her a rumbling belly. She yawned, fidgeted, did some grooming, then sprang up. She looked at Linda who was fast asleep as usual in her chair. Mimi saw that the door was only pushed too and not properly closed. She tiptoed round and jumped up onto Linda's desk. She stared down at the keypad on her laptop. Oh no! Her tail twitched, then it twitched again.

CHAPTER 8

Gunner and Sheba were chasing each other up and down Dragon Hill.

'Hey Sheebs, it's great to have you back again. I did miss you. Let's do jokes. Let's do fish jokes!'

'Oh, go on then. Why did the fish blush?'

'I know this one, it's erm...'

'Because it saw the ocean's bottom. Ha ha.'

'Oh, that joke is so old, Sheba.' The two cats crossed the road and leapt up into the cherry tree just opposite Mimi's house.

'Good cod, look over there.'

'Ha! Oh, stop with the fish jokes now Gunner, they're giving me a haddock!'

'Sorry Sheebs, I was being shellfish.' Gunner stared down at the little black cat trotting up the hill. 'That's odd...'

'What's odd, Gunner?'

'That looks like Mimi coming towards us, but she's supposed to be at Linda's Luxury Cat Hotel.'

Mimi spotted Gunner and Sheba up in the cherry tree.

'Hey Gunner!' she called out.

'I thought you were at Linda's for another week?'

'Well, I should be, but there was this incident...' she said, lowering her head. Gunner and Sheba jumped down from the tree.

'You remember Mimi don't you, Sheba?'

'Of course, I do.'

'What you see is what you get,' blurted out Mimi. Sheba looked puzzled.

'What do you mean, what you see is what

you get?' asked Gunner.

'It's a Shakespeare quote. I heard Linda say it.'

Gunner shook his head. 'No, I'm afraid not Mims. So, what happened?'

'Well, I suppose you could call it a 'good news, bad news' story, or actually, now I come to think of it, it's more like a 'bad news, worse news' story.'

'Oh, I see. It's as bad as that is it?'

'Well, all was going fine. Oh, and, I sort of made some new friends but I decided to stay away as I…"

Sheba pretended to yawn.

'Sorry, I'll get to the point.'

'Did your tail start to twitch?' asked Gunner. Mimi nodded.

'I was on Linda's desk you see, and looking down at the keypad, when I felt the urge, you know, the uncontrollable urge to be naughty. I don't know what came over me, but my paw just plonked itself onto the keys and that's when it happened. My claws shot out and I started to pick the letters off, one by one. They came off so easily. I flicked them up into the air and before I knew it, I'd picked off all the keys, all except one. I just couldn't get my claw underneath that one. It was well and truly stuck. Anyway, Linda phoned Lou and Simon to come and fetch me. She handed Lou my food and snacks, saying I wasn't allowed to go back to the hotel again – ever! When we got home, Lou shouted at me too! She said if I didn't bring them back immediately, I'd be in serious trouble! I don't know what came over me. I'm not usually naughty at Linda's. Oh Gunner, it's getting worse!' Mimi stared at the ground. She looked most upset.

'Don't worry Mimi. We'll think of something, you'll see,' said Gunner. 'But what did Lou mean Gunner, bring what back immediately?'

'Well, you've obviously stolen something of Lou's and you need to give it back, immediately!' snapped Sheba, with a disapproving glare.

'But I haven't stolen anything! You believe me, don't you Gunner?'

Gunner didn't sleep at all well that night; he was worried about Mimi.

The following day, Gunner trotted up the hill and stopped outside Mimi's house. The postman had arrived. But it wasn't Harry today. Everyone liked Harry the postman. He was jolly, said 'good morning' to everyone and always took the time to bend down and stroke the cats and dogs on Dragon Hill. Harry liked to tickle Gunner under the chin and make a fuss of him.

But it was Maureen today and Gunner didn't like Maureen. She was permanently grumpy and didn't like cats. He definitely wouldn't be getting a stroke this morning. He couldn't even remember a time when he had seen her smile. He ran over to her anyway, just in case she was in a happy mood, but her smile was most definitely upside down.

'Out of my way, cat!' she scolded and brushed past Gunner, knocking him into the road. Maureen started to march down Mimi's path. Gunner's eyes were drawn to the bright-green shrub near the front door. It seemed to be moving. Yes, it was definitely trembling. He edged a bit closer. This looked familiar.

He'd seen something like this before. And there it was, the unmistakeable black tail of Mimi, moving excitedly from underneath it.

'Hey Gunner! What are you doing here?' whispered Sheba, who had now joined him near the gate. 'Oh, my goodness Gunner, your cyst is so huge now. I could hang my coat on it!'

'Shush! Stop staring at my leg Sheba and watch this.'

'Oh no, you're not going to include me in one of your crazy schemes, are you?'

Sheba's eyes grew big as she stared at the shrub that was now shaking, and the black tail that was twitching rapidly from side to side. As Maureen walked past, Mimi shot out from underneath the shrub and leapt up at her, landing heavily on her shoulder.

Maureen shrieked. 'Get off cat!' she

shouted, scattering letters all over the lawn. But Mimi clung on tight with her long claws.

'Mimi! Get off now!' ordered Gunner. But his words went unheard.

Maureen was now running back down the path and up Dragon Hill. 'Get off of me you devil cat!'

Mimi was still clinging on, tighter than ever! Gunner caught a glimpse of her mischievous eyes. He also saw a scratch on Maureen's face. Was that blood? Oh dear! This wasn't going to end well!

'Well, Sheebs, I don't think there is anything we can do here. Who knew how much trouble a little black cat could cause?' he said. 'Hey look, here comes Darth.'

Darth came running up and stopped just in front of Gunner. He stared at Gunner's leg and shook his head.

'Massive cyst alert!' Visit to the vet for one.'

'Stop nagging, you're as bad as Sheba, and it's not a cyst as you all keep telling me. It's Jimmy!' Gunner added grumpily.

'But Darth's right, Gunner. You're going to have to show it to your owners. How did you do it anyway?' asked Sheba. 'Did you catch it on that sharp bit of fence at the allotments? I bet you did. I'm always telling you to keep away from there, but you just don't listen to me, do you?'

'Actually Sheebs, I lost my balance and fell over when I was practicing the Riverdance.'

Darth sniggered. Sheba put her nose into the air and started to walk away. 'I can see I'm not wanted here. I have far better things to do with my time anyway.'

Later on that day, Sheba was walking home along Dragon Hill. She paused when she reached Mimi's house right at the top. What was going on here then? It sounded like hammering and sawing. Being as curious as any other cat, Sheba couldn't resist trotting down the path to find out where the noise was coming from.

Following the path around the side of the house and into the back garden she saw Simon, Mimi's owner, sawing a hole in the shed door. Sheba sneaked past and hid under the hedge. The loud noises of drilling and banging made her ears hurt. And now Lou, Mimi's other owner, was walking towards the shed with Mimi's basket and bowl!

That's not looking good, thought Sheba.

'Hey look, Darth, what's up with Sheba?' Gunner shouted.

Sheba was running towards them looking most anxious. 'Oh Gunner! I've been trying to find you!' she said panting.

'Why? What's happened?'

'We need an emergency meeting! And fast!'

'Darth and I will try and find Mimi,' said Gunner. 'You go and fetch Agatha, we'll meet back at the clubhouse.'

'We need to split up,' suggested Gunner. 'It'll be quicker that way. You go to the park and the allotments, I'll go up to Mimi's house.'

Darth bounded down to the park, he looked in all the obvious places, including underneath her favourite shrub. Nope, she wasn't there. He would try the allotments next.

Gunner headed towards Dragon Hill and up to Mimi's house. He searched all around her garden, inside the Wendy house and behind the vegetable patch. Nothing. He was sure he would find her in the greenhouse fast asleep on the orange jumper, but she wasn't there either. Gunner walked back down the path and crossed over the road. Where else could she be? He heard a rustle from above. He looked up into the cherry tree. And there, right up high on the branch furthest away, was Mimi.

'There you are. We've been looking everywhere for you. Can you come down please – now!'

'No, I don't want to.'

'Don't make me come up and get you.'

Mimi thought about it for a few moments. 'Okay, I'll come down.' She climbed down through the branches and reluctantly walked over to Gunner.

'Why were you hiding in the tree, Mimi?'

'Well… I've been naughty again,' she mumbled, whilst hanging her head low.

'I know you have. We saw what you did to Maureen the postwoman.'

'I'm not allowed in the house anymore, not since the most recent incident.'

'You mean there's something else?'

gasped Gunner.

Mimi nodded.

'You're impossible. What did you do this time?'

'Well, you see, I accidently had an accident of the toilet kind, on Lou's new cushion.'

'You're lying Mimi, aren't you? It wasn't an accident, was it?'

'Okay, no. But hear me out.'

'Go on then.'

'I was angry with Lou and Simon. Have you seen what they've done?'

'I know, I just spotted it in the garden.'

'They're sending me to live in the shed!' wailed Mimi.

'Come on, let's get to the clubhouse, everyone is waiting.'

Mimi stopped just outside.

'Come on Mims, let's get inside.'

'But I don't want to Gunner, everyone will glare at me. Especially Sheba.'

'No, they won't. They're your friends. They just want to help you.'

Gunner walked into the room first. 'I found her everyone, she's here.'

Mimi followed and sat down next to Darth.

'May I start this meeting tonight?' asked Agatha, looking at each of the cats in turn. Gunner nodded.

'Sure thing,' said Darth.

'Well, if you must, but just this once,' said Sheba.

'Well,' began Agatha. 'It seems to me that an object or event of some kind is triggering something in Mimi which makes her disobedient.'

'Or just plain bad behaviour,' remarked Sheba.

'No wait,' said Agatha. 'I have it! We need to find the common denominator!'

'The common what?' asked Gunner.

'It's the common factor,' said Darth. 'The thing that connects it all together.'

'Well, we need to find this common thingamabob and fast!' said Gunner.'I fear it may be too late,' said Sheba. 'I just watched Lou put your basket and bowl in your new home Mimi. You're definitely in the shed.'

'There's nothing wrong with a shed,' said Darth. 'I spent my first few years in one. In fact, sometimes I miss it, especially when Ethan is coming after me with the hedgehog brush.'

'Well… after this Mimi, there is only one

place left to go,' added Sheba. 'THE CAT HOME!'

Darth narrowed his eyes at Sheba and glared. 'Don't you have an OFF switch?'

'That's enough of that,' interrupted Agatha. 'Now tell me, Mimi, has anything changed at home?'

'What do you mean, Agatha?'

'Has anything changed in your daily routine?'

Mimi frowned and thought for a moment. 'No, not that I can think of. I have the same meals, same flea drops, same basket, no, nothing has changed.'

Mimi looked around the room at her friends. 'I haven't always been this mischievous, you know. I was a perfectly normal cat once upon a time.'

'Hmm. I'm not going to give up on this idea, Mimi. There must be SOMETHING!' said Agatha.

'Well, you can all stay here and try to figure it out,' said Mimi, 'but I have to get back. I need to sort out my new home. And, as Darth pointed out, the shed will be good enough, so please don't feel sorry for me. At least it's not the cat home... yet.'

CHAPTER 9

Mimi sighed as she fidgeted yet again. She tugged at her blanket, bringing it closer over her small black body. She just couldn't get comfortable. And it was cold. The shed smelt damp and it was dark and gloomy. The only patch of light was from the window in the cat flap. She tried to make out the unfamiliar shapes in her new cramped home. There were two bicycles – she had already hurt herself on one of the pedals. What was that large shape at the back? It must be the lawnmower. She watched a long-legged spider scuttle across the floor and disappear under the plastic sheeting. What else was under the sheeting? Mimi didn't want to go and find out.

Just then the cat flap swung open and

a furry ginger head with pale green eyes poked his head through. 'Got any room for your favourite cool neighbour?'

'Oh Gunner!' purred Mimi, most relieved to see her friend. 'There's plenty of room in this basket. It used to belong to Wolfie next door, so it still has a doggie smell. I must warn you, it's not very comfortable in here.'

'This will do just fine,' he said. Though he wondered what the hard lump was under the basket. 'I thought you might like some company tonight, seeing as it's your first night in your new home.'

'That's very kind of you Gunner. I'll get used to it. Here, have some blanket.'

The two friends fidgeted some more before their eyelids started to get heavy.

'Look, there's a hole up there in the roof, Mimi. Can you see that big star. That means you can make a wish. You mustn't tell me what it is, although I can probably guess.'

'Tell me something,' asked Mimi. 'Why is this street called Dragon Hill?'

'Agatha said that there was once a huge dragon that lived at the top, just near here in fact.'

'Golly! I hope he's not still around.'

'Apparently, he was a nice dragon, Mims. He kept everyone warm one winter when it snowed for three months.'

'Wow, I'm getting sleepy now, but I feel warm and cosy, as if the dragon has warmed up the street again.'

'Time for sleep, Mimi.'

'Oh, I forgot to say, failure is not an option. It's a Shakespeare quote you know, Gunner.'

'Goodnight, Mimi.'

Gunner woke up early the next morning. After a big stretch he poked his head through the cat flap in Mimi's shed and smelt the fresh morning air. Mimi was still asleep but Gunner was an early riser. It was too early for breakfast but maybe he'd run up to Agatha's cottage and pop in and say hello. He stopped off at the skatepark and sat quietly on top of the hill and watched the big orange ball rise slowly up from behind the trees. It was time to get going.

He started with a gentle trot then galloped most of the way to Agatha's.He paused when he reached the garden path, breathing in the fumes from the lavender.

'Gunner! What a surprise! You're up early, you made me jump.'

'You're up early yourself, Agatha.'

'I just couldn't sleep. I've been thinking

about Mimi. I wish I could work out what has changed. We need to do something or we'll lose little Mimi. As Shakespeare once said, Nothing will come of nothing.'

CHAPTER 10

Sheba and Darth were chatting at the clubhouse.

'So Sheebs – is it alright to call you that by the way?'

'I'd rather you stuck to Sheba, my actual name.'

'Do you fancy a quick game of hide-and-seek then, Sheba? Nobody has ever beaten me. I remain the king of hiding around here.'

Sheba couldn't resist the challenge. 'Oh, go on then, but I had better warn you Darth, hide-and-seek is something I'm rather good at too.'

Darth counted to twenty slowly. 'Ready or not, here I come!'

Gunner pushed his head through the cat

flap of Mimi's new home but there was no Mimi. Where had she gone now?

He moved over to her bowl. She had eaten her breakfast. Well, most of it. There were just a few odd-looking snacks left. Gunner sniffed them. The smell of them made his mouth turn down at the corners. He suddenly looked up and gasped!

Gunner bounded up to the clubhouse. He couldn't wait to tell the others what he had discovered. But what was happening?! A shiny new fire engine was parked nearby and there were one, two, no, three fire fighters standing around and staring up at the tall oak tree. Gunner edged his way nearer to see what was going on. The engine's ladder was fully stretched and was leaning up against the top branch where the fourth fire fighter was. He was calling out something.

What was he saying?

'Come on puss, you can trust me, what's your name?'

Oh no! thought Gunner. What has Mimi done this time?

'It's Sheba, her name is Sheba,' called out one of the children from the skate park.

Gunner craned his neck back further. Sheba? What on earth was she doing? And why was she perilously perched on the top branch?

Gunner spotted Agatha trotting over to him.

'What's going on Agatha? Why is Sheba stuck at the top of the tree, she's never attempted that before.'

'Darth challenged her to a game of hide-and-seek and for some reason she thought it would be a great idea to hide in the oak tree. I tried to get her to come down but she insisted that it was none of my business and she just climbed even higher!'

'Oh dear,' said Gunner, biting his lip. 'The wind seems to have got up now too, that's not good.'

The cats, the children from the skate park and the neighbours from Dragon Hill had all now come out to watch. Gunner's owners came over carrying trays of tea and cake for the firefighters.

'I think he's nearly got her, Gunner!' cried Agatha, staring up at the firefighter at the top of the ladder. But as he tried to grab her, Sheba hissed at him and he missed. There were 'oohs' and gasps from the audience looking on until eventually Sheba, accepting defeat, leapt onto the firefighter. He held on to her tightly. Then carefully, one rung at a time, he stepped down the ladder and released Sheba safely onto the ground. There was a round of applause from everyone.

Gunner shook his head. 'What on earth were you thinking, Sheba? Look at all this chaos you've caused.'

'And let's not forget how dangerous that was for everyone,' scolded Agatha.

'It was dangerous for me too,' whined Sheba, looking at the ground in embarrassment. She quickly groomed her tail. Everyone watched as the firefighters packed away their ladder and waved as they drove away.

'Anyway Sheba, that was a very silly and dangerous game to play. Thank goodness it's over,' said Gunner.

'But… it's far from over. I have to find Darth – he hasn't won yet you know. Come on everyone, let's find him, he can't be far.'

Mimi came rushing over. 'Hey everyone, I've got such exciting news for you all!'

'I'm sorry to disappoint you Mims but I'm afraid it's gonna have to wait. We have to find Darth before it gets dark.'

Mimi sighed. 'Okay Gunner, all hands to the deck. Actually, I think that's a Shakespeare quote, in fact, I'm pretty sure it is.'

Two hours later and the cats had all returned to the clubhouse. They had looked in all the obvious places and had exhausted all possible places that a cat could hide.

'Do you think he's got stuck down a rabbit hole?' asked Gunner.

'No, definitely not,' replied Agatha, 'he wouldn't be that silly.'

'I wouldn't be so sure about that,' said Sheba.

'Now, let's think hard about this. Darth is definitely not here,' said Agatha. 'So that means he's in trouble!'

'I've been calling his name for ages, now,' added Mimi. 'He would have answered if he were here, I'm sure of it. Poor Darth, he must be frightened. How are we going to help him if we don't know where he is?'

CHAPTER 11

Over at the fire station on the outskirts of town, the firefighters were enjoying a mug of tea and a biscuit in the mess room. They were laughing and telling jokes. They were laughing so much that they couldn't hear meowing. Trapped inside the cupboard on the back of the fire engine was... Darth.

He had been meowing for two hours now and his voice was getting fainter. He was hungry, thirsty and scared. What if they don't find me for days! he thought. I wish that I hadn't been so silly. And little Ethan and Gracie will be so upset that I'm missing.

Darth's leg had now gone to sleep and he couldn't feel it any more. He tried meowing again, but the only noise that came out of his mouth was a croak. Nobody heard and nobody came.

'Are you sure about this, Gunner?' asked Sheba as they trotted along Church Street.

'Gunner's right, Sheba,' replied Agatha. 'We searched high and low for Darth, we have to try this.'

'I agree with Agatha,' said Mimi, 'and it's not far now, just over the road and round the corner. I remember passing the building on my way to Linda's.'

Gunner, Agatha, Sheba and Mimi found a safe place to cross the road. Two minutes later they stood outside the fire station. 'There,' said Mimi. 'I knew it wasn't far.' The daylight had now gone and it was almost dark. Gunner could see a door had been left just ajar.

'I'll go in first then give you the nod.' Gunner poked his head around the door. He could hear voices in the next room. He put his paw up and the other cats tiptoed in. 'The firefighters are in the next room everyone, they've just started a game of billiards or snooker. I'm not sure which it is, I always get the two mixed up.'

Agatha and Mimi had already run across the room and into the main station where there were two fire engines parked up. The other cats appeared. 'I think it was this truck, Gunner. I recognise it,' said Sheba.

'No, it definitely isn't that one Sheebs. It's this one, the new one with the big ladder.'

'No Gunner, you're wrong, it's this one and I should know. I had a bird's eye view of it, remember!' Sheba's tail was now wagging fast. She was getting angry. Sheba and Gunner continued to argue. Agatha stepped in.

'For goodness sake you two, what is this? Game of moans? Come on now, let's try and find Darth, time is of the essence.'

Mimi walked around the first fire engine calling his name. 'I don't think he's here; he would have answered if he was.'

Gunner walked over to the small door at the back of the fire engine.

'This is interesting everyone. Help me pull it open.'

Agatha and Mimi helped Gunner pull the door as hard as they could with their paws. After one last heave, it opened and there, trapped behind the fire blanket and looking out with his sad green eyes, was Darth.

'We found him Sheba! He's here!' shouted Gunner.

Darth climbed down slowly. 'How on earth did you find me guys? Listen, I've lost my voice.' Darth tried to meow but all that came out was a squeak.

'Now, let's try and get out of here without being spotted,' said Agatha.

The cats took a slow but steady walk in the dark, towards home.

'It's not too far Darth,' said Gunner.

'The walk will do me good guys. Being holed up in that tiny space for such a long time – I thought I was a goner!'

'Well, you're safe now,' said Agatha. 'Let's get back to the clubhouse.'

Agatha, Mimi and Gunner decided to stay with Darth that night.

'Are you staying too, Sheba?' Gunner asked.

'No. I always like to be in my own bed, but tomorrow I shall return and deal with Darth, in a non-violent manner of course.'

The next day, after the cats had been home for breakfast, they met back up at the clubhouse. All except one – Sheba. Agatha, Gunner and Mimi sat staring at Darth who was perched in the middle of the gold chair.

'So, what happened yesterday, Darth? We're all itching to know,' asked Gunner.

'Yes, I couldn't sleep,' said Mimi, 'but that's because of the exciting news I want to share with you all.'

'Well,' began Darth. 'I was looking for an original place to hide, because, that is the secret of hide-and-seek, you see. And I thought as everyone was busy watching Sheba being rescued from the tree, they wouldn't notice me. I saw the open cupboard on the back of the fire engine. I jumped in thinking how clever I had been, when one of the firefighters slammed the door shut and they drove off!

'I tried to get out but I couldn't. I meowed all night but nobody heard me. And then, dozens of Stormtroopers came marching down the ramp!'

'Are you sure that's right, Darth?' quizzed Gunner.

'Oh, no wait, I actually might have dreamt that bit.'

'You were very brave, Darth,' said Mimi.

'I'm not really brave, I'm just not very good at estimating risk.'

'Yes,' added Agatha, 'something you must do if you're a cat. I bet Ethan and Gracie were pleased to see you, Darth?'

'Oh yes, they certainly were, Agatha. When I saw their sad faces, I felt bad. They've been so good to me. They took me in when I wasn't wanted. I'm looking forward to going home and having my fur brushed, and I even don't mind a bit if Gracie wants to push me around in her pram. It's a great form of transport you know, especially if you're feeling a bit lazy.'

'Do you think Gracie would let me have a ride in the pram, Garth? It sounds like fun,' said Mimi.

There was a thump in the kitchen. Sheba walked in.

'I see you've got over your ordeal, Darth. I don't want to upset you, but I actually did win hide-and-seek yesterday.' Sheba jumped on to the gold chair and edged Darth off on to the floor.

'Actually, Sheba, I think you'll find that I was the clear winner,' said Darth, giving Sheba a wink.

Sheba shook her head. 'No, Darth, I won. The rules clearly state that you must be within fifty metres of the clubhouse.'

'No Sheebs, it's a hundred and fifty metres, so I won, without a doubt.' Darth winked at Sheba again.

'Will you stop doing that?'

'Doing what Sheebs?' teased Darth, winking again.

'If you don't stop, I'll shove you in that tiny drawer.'

'But I wouldn't fit!'

'Oh yes, you will!'

'Now that's enough of that, you two,' called out Agatha. 'There will be no winners. Hide-and-seek is over. It is cancelled due to ridiculous hiding places. And my decision is final. Now let's move on. We have far more important things to talk about.'

'Here here. I think it's time that we listened to Mimi,' called out Gunner. 'She has some very exciting news for us, don't you, Mims?'

'At last! I do indeed, and I've been bursting to tell everyone. I think you know what it is too, Gunner, don't you?'

'Well, this is exciting Mimi, do tell us!' said Agatha. 'But first, you need to sit on the gold chair.' Sheba reluctantly moved off.

'I think I'm done here anyway, I may go home,' said Sheba.

'But you can't go now, Sheba! Mimi is going to tell us her exciting news!' said Gunner.

'I know, I know, it's exciting,' said Sheba, rolling her eyes. 'I am prepared to jump up and down if necessary, okay?'

Mimi cleared her throat.

'Well, everyone, you just won't believe this, but I've worked out what the common denominator is! I know what's making me so mischievous! I thought about what Agatha said and there is this one small thing, it may not be anything at all, but…'

'What, Mimi?' said Agatha, anxiously tapping her claws on the floor.

'One of the things I love most, well I say love, I mean loved, was my Tricky Treats. They were the tastiest snacks ever, you just wouldn't…'

'Oh, just get on with it Mimi,' said Sheba, wagging her tail.

'Well, here's the thing. A while ago, Simon and Lou stopped giving me Tricky Treats. Instead, they gave me Lickie-Licious. Apparently, they cost a lot less than Tricky Treats. You can get a huge sack of them for next to nothing and...' Mimi looked embarrassed '...Lou and Simon are, I'm afraid to say, a bit on the stingy side.'

'She's right everyone,' piped up Sheba. 'You should see her bowl. It's so cheap and nasty, you wouldn't get me eating out of a thing like that.'

'So, do you really think that it could be the Lickie-Licious snacks which have been causing all the trouble? I saw the treats in Mimi's shed,' said Gunner.

'But...,' added Sheba. 'Let's not be

so hasty, you had a mischievous incident at Linda's Luxury Cat Hotel if I remember correctly.'

'I was eating my own food at Linda's. Lou and Simon brought it from home.'

'What do the Lickie-Licious snacks taste like?' asked Gunner.

'They taste most odd, and there's definitely a lot more chewing involved. I can't quite put my finger on what the flavour is, but there is a bitter aftertaste. It's something I haven't tasted before.'

'Or smelt before,' added Gunner, pulling a face.

'Well, you mustn't eat them anymore,' said Agatha. 'Who knows what else is in them.'

'Probably all the crumbs and broken bits swept up from the floor of the Tricky Treats factory plus a few rat droppings added to fill up the box,' said Sheba.

Mimi swallowed uncomfortably.

'Well, it couldn't be easier, Mimi. Just stop eating those nasty little treats,' said Gunner.

'But I don't want to upset Simon and Lou anymore.'

'Mimi! You have to stop eating them. Right away!' said Agatha. 'I insist upon it.'

'Well, you've done it, Mims. You've solved the case, just like a true detective. She shoots, she scores!' shouted Gunner as he leapt high into the air.

'Take it easy Gunner, Jimmy could burst at any time!' called out Darth.

'Right then,' said Agatha. 'We'll meet back here in two weeks. Mimi, you can report back to us. Let's hope that there will be no more incidents.'

'But there's something else too,' added Mimi. 'Do you remember that Lou kept telling me to put it back, then put them back?'

Gunner and Sheba both nodded.

'Well, Lou and Simon were going crazy the other night, they were searching the house from top to bottom. Sofa cushions were scattered everywhere, drawers were pulled out and frantically searched. Coat pockets turned inside out, with tissues flying everywhere. They even searched the freezer drawer! In the end it looked like a tornado had swept through the house.'

'But then what happened?'

'There was a visit from those annoying humans.'

'You mean Claude?' asked Agatha.

'Yes, him! He turned up with his owners, and you'll never guess what? He was made to hand his favourite bag over to Lou!'

'What was in it?' asked Sheba.

'Well, there were two television thingamabobs.'

'I think you mean remote controls,' said Sheba.

'Yes, that's what I said.'

'And?' said Gunner impatiently.

'Lou's car keys and her mobile phone! She couldn't find it anywhere, so she rang the number. Claude's owners were most shocked when they heard a phone ringing from under his bed!'

'Well, that's all well and good,' interrupted Sheba, 'but I... actually, have some rather exciting news myself,' she said, now grooming her paw.

All the cats looked on.

'What's that then, Sheebs? Tell us your news,' asked Gunner.

'My owners are going back to France, just outside of Paris to be exact, back to the holiday chateau for three months… and as I've been so well behaved, I'm allowed to go too!'

'But, don't you want to stay here with us?' asked Gunner. 'I'm sure it'll be more fun.'

Sheba shook her head. 'To be honest Gunner, this stopped being fun for me a while ago. And besides, I just can't wait to get back to Paris, darling. Must go and pack my things. Now, whatever shall I wear?' she muttered as she trotted out of the clubhouse.

'Oh, bye then Sheebs,' said Mimi. 'When

do you leave?'

Sheba didn't answer, she was already half way home.

CHAPTER 12

Two weeks later and early one morning, Mimi rushed over to Gunner's.

'Can you believe that I haven't been mischievous for over two weeks now. Can you believe that Gunner?'

'And can you believe that those little biscuits caused all that trouble? I'm so pleased we figured it out, Mims.'

'And you don't need to worry about me anymore, Gunner.'

'But there must be something to worry about?'

'Well, actually, it's probably nothing, but... let's get over to Agatha's first, I can't wait to tell her. And Simon and Lou keep picking me up and cuddling me. They've even let me back in the house.'

'I quite liked your shed though, Mimi, it was cool. You had Mr Spider for company and me for entertainment, and even your own little front door! Anyway, what was it that you wanted to tell me, Mims?'

'Well, I expect it's nothing to worry about, but when Lou realised, I'd stopped eating the Lickie-Licious treats, she collected them all up and put them in a bag and took them down to Sheba's house. She said she didn't want them to go to waste. You don't think Sheba would eat them do you, Gunner?'

'Nah, I'm sure she wouldn't. Anyway, she's setting off for France today, so she will be most excited. I'm going over there now to say bye to her, or rather au revoir.'

Mimi raced over to Agatha's while Gunner trotted across the road to find Sheba. There seemed to be a lot of noise and commotion coming from Sheba's driveway. Why were her owners shouting at the tops of their voices like that? What on earth was going on?

'What do you mean Michael, you can't get into the car?'

'It's Sheba! She's in the car and won't let me in! She's locked all the doors and now she's sitting in the driving seat! I think she's going to drive off!'

Oh dear, thought Gunner. Too late…

Agatha was sitting by the lavender. 'Mimi! Come and tell me, what's the verdict?' asked Agatha.

'Well,' said Mimi, panting. 'I am very happy indeed to report that giving up the Lickie-Licious treats seems to have cured me. I haven't done anything mischievous in over two weeks.'

'Fantastic news Mimi!' said Agatha. 'But where's Gunner?'

'That's strange, he should have been here by now, he was just going to say goodbye to Sheba then head over. I wonder what's happened to him?'

Two hours later, Mimi and Agatha were fast asleep by the lavender in the garden.

'Hey guys, wake up! It's me, sorry I'm late. They got me!' puffed Gunner.

Agatha and Mimi woke up with a start. They watched Gunner limp over the lawn to meet them.

'Who got you Gunner? And why are you limping?' asked Mimi.

Agatha looked at Gunner's leg. 'Your cyst, it's gone!'

'I was over at Sheba's when my owners came to meet me. They were so cunning. They enticed me into the kitchen with a delicious smelling breakfast… but then they cornered me and pushed me into the cat carrier and whisked me off to the vets!'

Mimi gasped. 'Oh, my goodness, Gunner!'

'I was so brave though, guys. I wish you could have seen. The vet attacked me with this massive needle and….'

'Okay Gunner, spare us the gory details,'

said Agatha, pulling a face.

'And then I had to have another injection so that I wouldn't get an infection.'

'Wow Gunner! Two jabs, you were very brave,' said Mimi.

'I know, but I miss Jimmy in a way. He was with me for quite a while, you know.'

'Anyway Gunner,' interrupted Agatha. 'Did you manage to say goodbye to Sheba before she left?'

'Erm... no. Didn't need to. Turns out Sheba probably won't be visiting France this time.'

'Oh, why ever not?'

'I'll tell you later, it's a bit of a long story. Come on guys, let's go down to the skatepark. No need to rush though, my leg is still a bit sore.'

Agatha and Mimi strolled along the

pavement towards the skatepark with Gunner limping behind. He was relieved to finally arrive.

'Look! Here comes Darth,' said Mimi. 'Look at his coat gleaming in the sunshine.'

'Wow Darth! Your coat looks amazing. Did Ethan use the hedgehog brush? And did it hurt?' asked Gunner.

'It wasn't too bad. I'm just relieved that the matted lumps have gone. My coat is so easy to clean now.' Darth gave his coat a quick lick.

The cats sat and enjoyed watching the children perform their flips and tricks for a while.

Mimi was very happy that morning. She ran two laps around the skate park then jumped up onto the high wall. She looked over at the other cats and called out:

'My horse, my horse, my kingdom for a horse! '

Gunner, Agatha and Darth all looked on with shocked faces.

'Why are you all looking so surprised?' said Mimi. 'Anyone would think that I'd just recited Shakespeare!'

'You did Mimi, you just did!' laughed Gunner.

The end

Other books in this series
by Sue Holland

He's Back

The Russian Princess

Sue Holland

MISCHIEVOUS MIMI

Sue Holland

Printed in Great Britain
by Amazon

80802387R00066